A Freeuse Hall Pass

A First Time Hotwife Story

Lacey Cross

CONTENTS

To all my readers who can't get enough of my freeuse resort stories—this one's for you. For everyone who's ever fantasized about being a wife shared by her husband with countless eager men, or dreamed of being that lucky hubby watching your wife fulfill her wildest desires, this steamy story is dedicated to you.

So get cozy and prepare for the ride of your life at the resort where anything goes and no craving is left unfulfilled. Things are about to get deliciously depraved...

CHAPTER 1

"Here's your room key card, Ms. Sinclair."

I bring my attention back to the perky woman checking me into the private Maui resort. She's holding a plastic room key out with a huge smile, and I take it from her. "Thanks."

"Will it be just you with us this weekend?"

"Yep, just me."

My husband, Quentin, booked us a three-night stay at a private resort on Maui. This resort is so private it's not listed in any travel brochures, and you basically need to know someone to get a reservation. Quentin's partner at work told him about it and hooked us up for a weekend getaway... only now I'm here alone because of a stupid work emergency.

The woman slides a printed brochure along the counter and starts talking about the resort's amenities. I've lived in Hawaii my entire life, and I tune her out as two sexy guys walking past catch my eye. They're in their 30s, tan and fit, wearing white button-down linen shirts and shorts. Mmm, maybe this is just what I need to recharge. I've always had an incredibly vivid fantasy life. I can relax and enjoy the eye candy and daydream about what I'd do if I had multiple guys to play with.

I glance at the woman and realize her mouth is still moving. I should be listening, but I just want to escape into a book and drink fruity alcoholic beverages with umbrellas while I think about getting all my holes filled at once.

She finally stops talking and beams at me. "If you have questions or need anything, feel free to ask for me personally. You can reach me via the main number, and I'll do whatever I can to help."

Her name badge says she goes by 'Joy,' which fits her sunny disposition. She seems genuinely excited about my stay despite the fact my husband can't join me, so I smile. "Thank you, Joy."

"You're welcome!" she chirps. "Read over the event details in the packet in your room if you decide to participate."

I have no idea what event she's talking about, but I'm not interested unless it involves me in a lounge chair by the pool admiring a ton of wet, hard bodies. I gather my luggage and give her a final smile before heading to my bungalow.

The resort is gorgeous, and I slow down to enjoy the walk. The landscaping is immaculate, and the entire property brings me a sense of peace. It seems more like a wellness retreat than your standard beachfront hotel.

The bungalow is a single room, but it's huge and luxurious, with a massive king-size bed, a large bathroom, a kitchenette, and a private terrace that faces out toward the ocean. I drop my bag and walk out the back sliding door. I can smell briny ocean salt in the air as I stroll down a winding stone path. There's another smaller building that I'm assuming is a sauna next to an outdoor pool surrounded by lounge chairs, a bar, and a cabana. Hell yeah, that's where I'll be all weekend.

I wander down another path until it leads me to an expansive golden beach. I slip off my sandals, dig my bare feet down into the warm sand, and breathe in the tropical air as I stare out at the blue water. Damn, I wish Quentin was here. This was going to be an epic fuckfest weekend after several busy months. He's been putting long hours in at work, and we haven't had as much headboard banging against the wall as I need.

I sigh. Well...he's promised me a romantic night when I get back with a nice dinner while I tell him all about the trip. I'll work up an appetite by enjoying the...scenery...before I come home. Thinking about the yummy guys I saw at check-in makes my body hum with a low level of desire, and I daydream some more about how this weekend could have gone with Quentin as I spend an hour wandering the beach and then exploring the lush grounds.

When the sun starts to set, I go back to the bungalow, feeling a little lonely. Damn, this just isn't as much fun without Quentin. I really wish I was getting all the sex he's been promising me for weeks. Ugh, there's no sense in dwelling on it. I'm determined to be happy and relax on the trip.

I've always had a higher sex drive than Quentin. Over the years, we've talked about opening our marriage up for me to play with other guys, but I've never really felt the need. My husband and my battery-operated boyfriend, when

Quentin is busy, have served me well. Doesn't mean I don't still fantasize about fucking other guys, though.

As I unpack my suitcase, I think about what my crazy husband said last night. He joked that he could make arrangements for me to get some action at the resort because he loves me that much. He's a total goofball. How was he going to make a guy who wants to fuck me magically appear with only one day's notice?

Laughing at the memory of our conversation, I pull my e-reader from my luggage and set it on a packet of information that the resort left on the nightstand. I'll spend the rest of the night curled up reading spicy stories while the sea breeze comes in through the open windows. I even brought a few sex toys if I get in the mood...and I'm definitely feeling in the mood.

As I unpack, I think about my husband's offer—he called it a hall pass to make up for him working. Hmm, I wonder how many women actually fuck other men if their husbands allow it. I've read stories about wives cheating on their husbands while on vacation, but I wouldn't be cheating if I asked permission. But does any of this happen in real life? I mean, I know there are swingers' clubs and stuff, but I've never been interested in anything like that.

What guy wants to share his wife without asking for the same treatment to fuck other women?

I kick off my sandals and stretch out on the bed, crossing my ankles and admiring the red polish on my toes next to my golden-brown skin tone. My legs have always been my favorite feature. They're long and slender from years of playing tennis and swimming regularly. My ass is pretty good, too. Since I was expecting a bunch of sex this weekend, I'm waxed and soft in all the right places. I plan on wearing shorts or a bathing suit all weekend. I might be alone, but I'm going to feel damn sexy. If I catch someone checking me out, even better.

My phone lights up, and I can tell by the ringtone that it's my husband.

I smile as my stomach gives a happy flip, and I answer, "Hey babe."

His voice is low and smooth. "Hey beautiful. Are you settled in?"

"Yep, I am…" I give him my best fake pouty voice. "*All alone.*"

I can hear that he's outside, walking as he talks. "Are you in the bungalow?"

"Yeah, all checked in. Where are you?"

He sighs. "I'm heading to the car to go home."

I frown and pick at the hem of my shirt, wishing he was here. "It's lonely without you. Stupid work. Your partner should feel bad. We could have been having sex right now in this wonderfully soft bed."

"I know," he says with regret in his voice. "I'm really sorry, baby."

I don't want to ruin both our weekends, so I change the subject and tease him. "Well, I'm going to enjoy myself. I'm going to read a lot of books and relax...or maybe I'll just hang at the pool and flirt with a few guys."

Quentin laughs. "There'll be plenty of single men at the resort tomorrow. I wanted to ask you what you thought about the event."

He knew about that? "What's the event about?"

"You should have information on it. They told me all the information would be in the room."

Oh! I sit up in bed and grab the folder on the nightstand. "I haven't read it yet, but what's going on tomorrow?"

"It's a freeuse day at the resort. There's supposedly a wristband in the packet if you want to take part in it."

What the...suddenly I realize this is why he casually mentioned he saw something about freeuse a few weeks ago and explained what freeuse was. My entire body buzzes and my pussy tingles as I think of those sexy men again. I decide to play dumb and see what he says. "Wait...what does 'freeuse' refer to?"

"Remember? I looked it up online. It's where someone makes themselves available for whoever wants to fuck them. In this case, the resort has a day where the women wear a wristband that says any of the guys at the resort can fuck them."

I'm so horny my clit aches, but I need to verify he's really saying what I think he is. "So if I wear the wristband, any of the guys here can approach me and ask to have sex? Like...I'd be freeuse for them?"

"Yeah, though no one is going to ask. If the wristband is on, that means you're open for business and anyone can fuck you...if that's what you want to do," he suddenly sounds unsure, as if he doesn't know how I'm going to respond.

Holy shit! I'm already soaking wet at the idea of fucking a stranger or two...or three. "You'd be okay if I did this?"

"Yeah, I mean, it's totally up to you, but I thought it might be something that you'd be interested in." He chuckles and adds, "And...you know...I'm okay with it. Your hall pass is good for whatever you want to do this weekend."

Holy shit! My mind races with the possibilities, and I'm almost shaking with desire. I'm so aroused my nipples ache, and I squeeze my thighs together to relieve the tension. Oh god, I really am desperate for a cock. It's been several weeks since Quentin and I've had sex. I thought my sex toys would do, but now that I hear about a freeuse offer, I just need to fuck someone.

My voice sounds breathy when I speak again. "What if they run a train on my ass?"

He laughs. "Baby, if it happens, go wild."

"Are you serious?" I ask incredulously. This is a joke. I can't even process this right now.

I can tell he's amused. "Only if you want to, but baby...I want to know every detail. Every. Single. Detail." He pauses and I hear him breathing heavily like he's turned on.

"I'm okay with whatever you want to do. I love you, and I trust you completely. You know that."

Wow, he is serious. My entire body is flushed and hot at the prospect of fucking multiple guys in a row with no inhibitions or rules. I can't even wrap my mind around it. It sounds too good to be true, but I'm dying to explore.

He clears his throat. "I have to go now, baby. Keep me posted tomorrow if you decide to go for it. You can call whenever. I'll keep my phone on while I'm working."

I'm speechless, and my pussy is throbbing with need. I can hardly think of what to say, so I give a soft, "Uh huh."

I hear him laughing. "Have fun, baby. Love you." I echo back that I love him, and we disconnect.

Dropping the phone in my lap, I lie back and stare at the ceiling. Oh, my god...did my husband actually give me permission to fuck as many people as I want?

Needing to know the details, I quickly grab the paperwork and search for the section describing the upcoming event.

Welcome to Paradise!

The staff here at Maui's exclusive Freeuse Resort would like to welcome you. If you are reading this, that means you're interested in participating in the event.

Tomorrow, our resort will open our doors to all guests for the monthly Freeuse Day event.

Freeuse Day is a special event where our guests can participate in our unique brand of resort hospitality. We offer the opportunity for the enthusiastically consenting women to be used by the men visiting the resort for their enjoyment. Don't worry, the women report high levels of satisfaction in the exit surveys. If you choose to partake in tomorrow's festivities, slide one of the provided wristbands on to show your willingness.

Please note: the band is optional and is not mandatory for enjoying the resort during the day. No one will touch you if you don't have a band on, but this is a special weekend that most guests book months in advance for, so we encourage people to be open to the possibilities.

If you choose to wear the wristband, you agree to the terms below...

I scan the list of terms, and it goes into an explanation about how I can remove the wristband at any point, and if I am ever uncomfortable and want someone to stop, just say "red light," and all the guests are aware that they must stop. It has a detailed section about the screening process for the guys, and how most men are repeat visitors. It also states the men use the buddy system so that it's usually two or more men at a time.

Oh god, two men at a time...

My head is spinning by the time I read through it all. My husband knew about this, and he planned to surprise me all along with this offer. I think about this for a few moments and then giggle. Hah, I bet Quentin is super bummed he's going to miss out on seeing me railed by a bunch of guys. Whenever he and I talked about me becoming a hotwife, he said he'd like to see the look on my face as another guy fucked me. There's no way he booked a trip during a freeuse weekend without planning to watch.

I'm still in shock as I flip to the end of the packet and find a small pouch attached to the back cover. Inside are four different colored wristbands with a card explaining what each one is for. The pink wristband is for vaginal penetration, the purple for anal, and the black for oral. The card says I can wear multiple bands, but there's also a green wristband that means 'open,' for women who are willing to take it anywhere the guy wants to stick it.

My entire body shivers as I stare at the wristbands. I've fantasized for years about being gangbanged. I've watched porn where a group of guys use a girl for their own satisfaction, and it's the hottest, dirtiest thing I've found online. But the reality of actually having that happen? That seems impossible and unrealistic.

But...what would be the harm if I did? My husband gave me his permission, and it would be like a dream come true for me. No one knows me here. I can just pretend like it's some sort of roleplay. My pussy buzzes and my nipples ache while a restlessness overtakes me. Yeah, I'm doing it.

Now the only question is...what color wristband am I wearing tomorrow?

CHAPTER 2

When I wake up the next morning, I spring out of bed. I slept surprisingly well last night, given how long it took my brain to turn off. It was probably the bed. It was like sleeping on a cloud. I force myself to eat something from the breakfast options in the kitchenette; orange juice, a bagel with cream cheese, and some mixed fruit should be enough to keep me fueled until lunch.

My heart pounds in eagerness at the thought of being approached by a man and fucked. I'm nervous. It's been years since I've seen a cock other than my husband's, and now I'm contemplating letting a complete stranger fuck me in a public setting. It seems surreal.

After a quick shower, I put on a bikini and wrap myself in a robe before sitting in front of the vanity table to dry my long black hair. Once it's completely dry, I decide to style it in a loose braid in the back. I put the bare minimum on for makeup since I don't know how today will go. Something tells me it might be pointless to dress up too much. After applying some perfume, I step in front of the full-length mirror.

I'm only 5'3", but even so, my legs seem to stretch for days. I'm proud that I've always stayed in shape by playing so much tennis. I'm definitely a normal woman and have my flaws, but today, I'm excited and radiant. Nothing is going to stop me from enjoying myself.

The only thing left to do is call my husband and tell him what I'm doing and which color bands I'm choosing. As much as I'm turned on by the idea of a bunch of guys using me and taking me wherever they want, I don't think I'm ready for freeuse anal sex. That seems like jumping off the deep end, and I'm not quite that brave. I'll give the guys two holes to use. I can handle that.

I take a deep breath and dial Quentin's number.

When he answers, I blurt out, "I'm doing it."

Quentin chuckles, "Okay. So...what are you wearing to-day?"

I swallow nervously. "My black bikini."

"That's it?"

I giggle. "Yep, I figured it would make it easier for any guy who wants me."

Quentin growls, "Fuck baby...I'm so hard right now. I wish I could be there to see it."

I smile. "Me too. You'll be the first person I call after."

Quentin laughs. "So, which wristband color are you wearing?"

He sure knows a lot about how this freeuse day works. My pussy throbs at the thought of him planning this trip. He's probably been thinking about this for days. Stupid work. "Pink and black, so they can use my mouth or pussy."

My husband inhales sharply. "I want you to tell me every detail when you get home. Promise."

"I will, honey. I promise." A wave of love for him washes over me.

He sighs and asks in a quiet voice, "Are you scared, baby?"

I bite my lip. "No...I think I'm excited. Nervous...but mostly excited."

"Good," he replies. "You deserve to have a good time. Just relax and go with the flow. Have fun and let them use you. I know you're going to love this."

I smile. "What I know is that I love you."

"I love you so much, sweetheart. Go have fun and call me later."

We blow kisses at each other over the phone before we disconnect.

I'm so lucky. He's the perfect husband for me. He understands and supports me in everything. I couldn't ask for anything more. But now it's time to strut my stuff around the resort and see what happens. My hands tremble as I slide the two colors of wristbands on and let them settle on my right wrist.

I stare at the bands for a moment, and my mind drifts to the first time I hooked up with Quentin. Usually the first time is a little awkward, but he knocked my socks off. He seemed to understand exactly what I needed. We're very compatible in bed—when we have time in our busy schedule—but I've always had a hard time orgasming. I wish I could just have a bunch of orgasms in a row until I'm exhausted...like those porn stars do in the movies where they fuck five or six guys in a row.

A sudden rush of arousal shoots through me. Oh my god, that is actually what I'm going to do today...and my husband approves. My nipples stiffen, and I rub my thighs together. Fuck, I hope they don't waste time talking and just get right to it.

I hope I get a bunch of orgasms.

My clit pulses in excitement. I'm so horny I can't stand it. I'm not sure if I'll be able to wait until someone approaches me. Can I approach the guys?

Shit, the sooner I get out there, the sooner I'll find out. It's time to check out the pool. I slather sunscreen on before grabbing my e-reader and a towel. The day is warm with a light breeze, and I breathe deeply. I'm ready to be a freeuse slut...whatever that entails.

I'm halfway to the pool when a thought almost makes me trip. Oh fuck, what if no one wants to have sex with me? What if the man to woman ratio is off and all the men are busy with other women? I shake my head. No, the resort wouldn't do that. Chances are I'm more likely to be one of the few women wearing wristbands. How many women actually come to this place?

When I get to the pool, it's deserted and my stomach drops in disappointment. Shit, where are the roaming pairs of men? I was expecting to see a bunch of guys waiting in line to fuck the first woman they saw. Where the hell is everyone?

I make my way to a chaise lounge chair and lay out my towel before settling in with my book to wait. I try to relax and read, but my mind races as I wonder where all the men are.

As I'm debating going to the beach, the sound of male laughter draws my attention. Two super sexy guys who are probably in their late 30s walk into the pool area. My pulse speeds up as they look at me. They're both fit with muscular builds. One of them has thick, muscular thighs, and I imagine he could plow a woman for a long time without breaking a sweat.

Butterflies swirl in my stomach as I wonder if they are going to come over here. I try to focus my eyes on my page, but I keep sneaking glances at them. They're both super sexy, and they're wearing matching blue trunks and have similar haircuts. The slightly shorter one has dimples when he smiles. Oh god, I love guys with dimples.

When Dimples looks my way and catches my eye, he smiles. My face flushes as I quickly turn my attention back to my book. I try to read another page, but my mind races as I wonder what's going to happen.

When I peek at him again, he's still watching me. He gives me a wink, and I feel a wave of desire. He needs to come over here and fuck me. My pussy is pulsing, and I'm so horny I can't think straight. I cross my legs and shift positions in a desperate search for relief.

The two guys approach me, and I have a moment of uncertainty. Wait, am I supposed to open my legs as soon as they get here? What's the protocol at a freeuse resort?

They stop next to my chair and Dimples smiles at me. "Hello...I'm Jared. You must be new at the resort."

"I'm Matt." His friend grins at me.

I swallow nervously. "I'm Alyssa."

Jared's dimples deepen. "Are you sure about that?" I'm confused and about to question him when he continues. "Or are you just a toy with no name?"

Time stands still for a moment while my mouth pops open and my entire body buzzes with an illicit thrill. No one has ever talked to me like this before, and if asked, I probably would have said I didn't like it...but goddamn, I like it.

Matt grabs my ankles and tugs me down the chaise lounge. I squeak and almost drop my e-reader.

Jared barks out, "Keep reading, slut. Don't mind us."

Don't mind them? I'm supposed to keep reading? I hold up my e-reader and try to focus on the screen as Jared spreads my legs and kneels between them. His hand slips underneath my bikini bottoms and fingers my pussy, and I gasp at the intrusion but continue pretending to read.

Jared's fingers stroke me, spreading my lips apart and sliding inside me. "Mmm...such a filthy slut. You're soaked already just by the thought of being used."

A zing of bliss swirls in my core from his fingers and his dirty talk. Holy fuck. I wanted someone to use me without wasting time on small talk, but I wasn't actually expecting it to happen.

Matt kneels next to the chair and shoves my bikini top up above my tits, exposing my nipples to the air. Matt cups my breasts, playing with the nipples before leaning over to take one into his mouth. I have to raise the e-reader higher and hold it in the air while Matt swirls his tongue around my nipple.

Every nerve in my body is lit up with pleasure as his skillful mouth makes the words blur on the page. I'm so distracted by Matt I don't realize that Jared has his cock out until I feel him push my bikini bottoms to the side and the tip of it presses against my pussy. I moan as Jared slowly pushes inside and stretches me open. Fuck, he's bigger than I expected, and the fullness makes my head spin as delight swirls in my core.

I try to keep reading, but it's difficult to concentrate on the words when Jared starts to fuck me. At first he's slow but then picks up his tempo. Each thrust sends ripples of ecstasy coursing through my entire body, and I'm moaning and crying out with every whack against my pussy.

Matt chuckles as he moves to the other breast and plays with the nipple with his fingers. "You've got great tits. I like how they bounce while he's fucking you."

As soon as he says that, I imagine what I look like. I'm spread open with my feet on the pavement while a guy kneels between my legs and fucks me. This is obscene.

I'm panting as I look at him and Jared, who's balls deep inside me now. I don't care how this looks, I want more. The pressure intensifies, building with each stroke. I'm so close...I just need something to send me over the edge.

A soft giggle distracts me for a moment as a couple walks past us and a woman murmurs. "Now that looks fun."

Ooooh, shit. There is another woman here. My mind reels knowing someone saw me spread out like this, but I can't think about it too long because Matt slides a hand down to my clit.

As he brushes circles around it, he says, "I know, let's have you read to us. Do it, now."

Oh fuck, I can't do that. I can't even form a sentence... plus I'm reading erotica. Jared's thrusts speed up and Matt rubs harder at my clit until the sensation overcomes any hesitation and I start reading the book out loud to them, my voice wobbling:

> "Have a seat, Miranda. We need to talk." Mr. Jacobs's voice is neutral, and he doesn't seem angry. The thought crossed my mind that he might fire me. I hope he fucks me first.

That's as far as I get before I can't speak. Matt's fingers on my sensitive nub send me flying, and I cry out as the orgasm tears through every nerve ending in my body. I buck my hips wildly as the violent orgasm peaks again and the waves of bliss crash over me.

I'm still gasping from the intensity of my release when I feel Jared tense as he pumps his cum deep into my pussy. He shudders and groans loudly as he collapses on top of me. We both lie there panting in a sweaty heap on the chair.

My e-reader is still in my hands, and I stare at the words on the screen, not really comprehending them. My brain is mush.

I lower the device and notice a small crowd of men has formed around us. A few guys stand nearby with their hard cocks out, stroking them. Matt stands and addresses the guys.

"Sorry boys, I called dibs on this one. You can play with her after." He winks at me, making me blush, right before he pulls me off the chair and carries me over to a nearby metal lattice table. I'm still clutching my e-reader, and he sets me down long enough to bend me over the surface. I gasp when my nipples come in contact with the cool metal.

Matt's voice is gruff. "Keep reading, slut. I was enjoying that story."

Oh fuck. I'm not sure I can read more—especially not with an audience. I take a moment to find where I left off:

> I sit down and cross my legs, letting my pencil
> skirt slide up past my knees.

Matt pulls my bikini bottoms down past my ass and I moan as he slams into me.

"More," he demands.

Shit...fuck...my voice trembles as I continue:

> Mr. Jacobs glances at my legs, so I know I hit
> my target with my chosen posture.

Matt goes into a frenzy, whacking against my pussy so hard the e-reader shakes too much to continue. This is so fucked up, but I love it. I want to beg him to never stop.

The world fades away as I immerse myself fully into the moment. I'm not sure how long he pounds into me, but when Matt's fingers find my clit, it sends me into the abyss.

Throwing my head back, I scream as I come all over his cock.

I hear him growl with pleasure, and I can feel hot spurts of cum shooting inside me. He grinds against my ass as he finishes. "Ah…yeah. So good."

I'm still trying to catch my breath when I hear a voice behind me. "My turn."

Before I have time to recover, Matt pulls out and another guy slides into my pussy. Who is this? I try to glance over my shoulder, but his strong hand pins me to the table while he hammers into me.

I cry out in bliss as he rams me mercilessly. My nipples are caught in the lattice of the table, and each thrust pulls at them, increasing my pleasure. The guy fucking me leans forward, and his voice is in my ears. "You like it rough like this?" he pants. "I bet you do…you're so wet. You've been dying for this, haven't you? Desperate to have your pussy pounded and filled with cum by strange men?"

I whimper. Oh, yes. Yes. I'm so turned on, it's unbelievable. I didn't even know I wanted this before last night, but this experience is amazing.

"Tell me you want to be our cumdumpster slut."

He's not wrong. I do want it, but I'm so lost in a fog of lust that it's hard to form the words. All I can do is chant, "Yes, yes, yes," as he hammers into me.

I'm completely at his mercy, surrendering to the thrill of being taken in front of an audience. He slides his hand under me and rubs my clit in tight, fast circles. The sensation is too much.

I explode, wracked with pleasure, and I barely understand what I'm saying as I cry out, "Yes! Fuck...please use me...I want it! I'm a cumdumpster. Use me however you want."

I'm a slut. I am. I'm so turned on I'd agree to anything they wanted me to do. The man fucking me roars, and I can feel his cock jerking inside me while he shoots his load. He pumps into me, fucking his cum back into me until he's done.

When he pulls out, I hear Matt's voice behind me. "Good job, babe. That's it for now."

Matt pats me on the ass and helps me stand. My knees wobble, and my head feels like it's going to float away on a cloud of bliss. I look around at the men surrounding me and give them all a loopy smile as I pull the bikini bottoms back into place.

I'm a little unsteady on my feet, but I manage to stand without falling over. "Thanks..." I mumble. I'm not sure how to end that statement. Thanks for using me? Thanks for the fuck? Thanks for the mind-blowing climaxes? I giggle. I guess it was all the above.

Jared smiles at me and holds up my e-reader. "You dropped this," he teases. He winks at me as he hands it over, and I giggle again.

"Have a good day, slut."

I nod and watch Matt walk away with Jared. This place is insane in the best of ways.

I'm still in a state of euphoria, and I can hardly believe what just happened. I just got fucked in a semi-public area by total strangers. Two of them introduced themselves, I guess, but I don't know who that third guy was.

A sudden need to talk to my husband hits me, and I adjust my bikini top, grab my stuff, and make a beeline for my bungalow. As I walk the paved path, I pull out my phone, check the time, and notice it's only been an hour since I last called my husband.

He answers immediately. His voice is husky, like he's turned on. "Hey, baby...did you just get started?"

I smile at his eagerness. "You could say that. I've had sex with three guys so far, and that was just the first hour."

Quentin laughs. "Wow...that's good work. How was it?"

I giggle at the absurdity of that statement. How was it...how was it? "Um...it was amazing."

Quentin chuckles. "Yeah? I knew you would love it. Did they call you dirty names?"

I laugh. "Yes, I got called a filthy slut, a cumdumpster...and maybe other stuff. I liked it."

Quentin groans. "Fuck...that's so hot. What's next on your list?"

I bite my lip and grin to myself. My husband is so naughty.

My mind flashes through what I want to happen next. "I want to get railed...hard."

Quentin's moan makes my clit throb, and he asks, "Do you want more than one guy at once, or one at a time?"

A shiver runs down my spine, and I whisper, "I want to be filled completely."

I can almost see my husband's face as he imagines multiple guys fucking me at the same time. I'm so focused on Quentin I squeak in surprise when someone pulls on the handle of my beach bag. I look over my shoulder and there are two guys behind me. One of them pulls me off the concrete path and into the grass before pressing on my shoulders.

I kneel and blink up at them. Uh…I'm on the phone. Can't they see that?

"Baby, are you still there?" My husband sounds worried.

"Yeah, I'm here. Two men just stopped me in the middle of the path and pushed me to my knees."

"Right now?" His voice is higher pitched than normal, like he's shocked.

"Yeah, I think…oh, one of them just pulled his cock out."

His voice is low. "Where's the other guy?"

"He's kneeling behind me."

"What's he doing?"

"I think he's…Oh fuck…" I whimper as he pushes me forward and I put my free hand down so I'm on my hands and knees, holding the phone with one hand and balancing my weight on the other.

When he yanks my bikini bottom down to my knees, I moan at how filthy this is to be talking to my husband on the phone while some guy is about to fuck me. I can hear Quentin's breathing becoming ragged.

I gasp when I feel the man's hands on my hips and he slides his massive cock into my pussy in one deep thrust. He's bigger than any of the guys who fucked me at the pool, and my vision blurs from the pleasure as he pings every nerve ending inside me.

I whimper, "Ohhh...he just slammed his cock into me."

Quentin groans. "Baby...fuck...that's hot. You have no idea what this is doing to me right now. How does it feel? Describe it to me."

I pant, "He's got a big cock, honey."

He groans, "How big?"

"So huge," I gasp out between thrusts. The guy is really pounding me. "Oh god...it feels incredible."

I'm so wet that I can hear him sliding into me with each thrust, which only adds to the excitement of being fucked while listening to Quentin's heavy breath in my ear.

His tone is insistent. "Tell me how much you like it."

I moan, "Oh, god. So amazing. I wish you were here so you could see this."

When the guy spanks my ass, I cry out and almost drop the phone. Fuck! The second guy stands above my head, jerking his cock, and I keep my eyes trained on his hand moving along his shaft. I lick my lips, anticipating tasting it. I open my mouth and stick my tongue out, hoping he'll blow his load on my face.

Quentin's breath stutters. "Oh, fuck..." he groans. "I can't believe I'm stuck at work."

The guy behind me slams into me repeatedly, and I can feel my tits swaying with each hard thrust. My pussy clenches at the thought of how much of a slut I am right now. The phone is pressed into my ear so hard it hurts, but I don't dare move as the guy behind me whacks against my pussy and the other guy jerks his cock inches from my face.

Quentin's voice is low. "Are you going to suck him off, baby? Let that guy cum in your pretty mouth?"

"Uh huh...I'm gonna swallow it," I whisper.

Quentin growls and the guy above me steps closer, his cock almost touching my face. I tilt my head up, keeping my tongue out and waiting for it.

Quentin groans. "Open wide for him, baby."

The guy in the back pounds my pussy harder, and the second guy aims his dick at my open mouth. He strokes himself furiously, and I watch with fascination.

It's so fucking hot to have my husband on the phone listening to this. The man jerking off over my face groans, and a huge load of cum splatters across my lips and tongue while the guy behind me continues to hammer me relentlessly.

I moan in pleasure as I taste the cum in my mouth and lick it from around my lips, swallowing it eagerly. The guy behind me grunts and gives a final cry as he jerks and blows his load deep inside me.

I'm on fire, and I want more. I need more...

The two guys are done, and the guy behind me stands up. Neither of them says anything as they adjust their cocks back into their pants and walk away.

My body vibrates from being fucked without coming, and then I realize I'm still on the phone. "Honey, you still there?"

Quentin chuckles. "Of course I am. I want to know how many loads of cum you have in you right now, baby girl."

"Four? I think...unless you count the guy who came over my face. But I didn't come just now. I'm still hungry for cock."

"You are?" he moans. "How do you want it, baby? Tell me."

I giggle. "First, I need to get back to my room before more guys find me."

My husband sighs. "Okay, shit. I really need to get back to work for a bit. Call me later with all the details, okay?"

"I will, sweetheart. Love you, bye."

"Love you too, bye."

I disconnect and pull myself up off the grass. I'm still shaky, but I manage not to fall as I pull on the bottom half of my bikini and stumble back to my cottage.

Once I get inside my room, I lock the door for privacy. I'm still dripping with the loads of cum the guys deposited inside me, and my thighs are covered in sticky residue. I'm also a little embarrassed at how slutty I acted. It wasn't just the other guys...Quentin got me all worked up with his comments and encouragement. Fuck, I'm so turned on right now, but I don't want to get myself off, so I decide to take a cool shower to calm down.

After my shower, I'm exhausted. I need some energy for this evening if I want the chance at more orgasms. I face plant on the bed, and within seconds, I'm out like a light.

Chapter 3

I sleep for a solid four hours, and when I wake up, I'm groggy and disoriented. Jesus. What a morning.

My stomach grumbles, and I slip a robe on and dig into the tiny fridge for more food. The resort has a dining room, and I should probably explore that later, but right now I don't want to risk some guys finding me before I get food in my belly. I can't wait to get pounded again. I'm so damn horny, and my pussy aches for a cock.

While I nibble on a cheese, meat, and fruit platter, I scroll through some social media posts and check out what my friends and family are doing this weekend. How would they react if they knew I was getting fucked by total strangers? I don't think anyone would believe what I've done. I really only have one friend I'm close enough to that

I'd tell about this adventure. Oooh, hell, I'm going to tell her now and see what she says.

I take a quick picture of the gorgeous view outside the open back door and message it to her.

Alyssa

The resort is gorgeous, but wait until you hear about the special event this weekend.

She responds immediately.

Mandy

Oh? Spill it.

Alyssa

There's a 'freeuse' day where the guys at the resort can fuck me all they want. Quentin told me to go wild and live my best life.

Mandy

What????? OMG! Are you fucking kidding me?

Alyssa

I'm not. I already had 5 different guys come on me or in me so far today.

FIVE? Holy shit. How do you feel?

I giggle, remembering this morning.

Amazing. I need to get back out there. I need another orgasm. I'll chat with you later and tell you all about it!

Go! Have fun! Be a super slut. I can't believe you're doing this, but I'm proud of you. You go, girl!

I laugh and set my phone down so I can finish my food before I head out. Just as I take a sip of water to wash down my last bite, there's a knock on the door. I jump, wondering who that is.

Pulling the robe closed, I quickly tie it tight before walking to the door. Right before I turn the handle, the knock comes again, and I hear my husband's voice call out, "Room service."

I squeal and yank open the door. My heart races as I launch myself into his arms. "Oh my god, you came!!!"

I'm so happy to see him. I pepper his face with kisses.

His body vibrates with laughter, and his voice is husky with emotion. "I couldn't stay away. I needed to be here to watch you. I told work they were going to just have to live without me."

My heart melts, and I can't stop grinning. Quentin gives me a devilish grin as he closes the door. I expect him to launch into questions about this morning, but I'm surprised when he spins me around and pushes me face first against the closest wall.

Oh, holy fuck. He's going to use me? Yes, please!

He grabs my wrists, pins them to the wall above my head, and leans forward so his mouth is near my ear.

My heart beats frantically as he whispers, "I thought of other men using you while I was at work, and then I re alized...you're mine. Why do they get to be the only ones who are having fun?"

I whimper as his free hand slips between my legs and his fingers slide inside my pussy.

"Fuck, baby...you're so ready for cock, aren't you? Do you know how hard it is to concentrate when all I can think about is fucking this sweet pussy?"

He's breathing heavily, and I push my butt back against his crotch and rub against his erection through his clothes.

Quentin groans, and his voice is thick with arousal. "You want me to fuck you right here against the wall?"

I don't answer him. It's his choice what he does with me. He's the one who told me how freeuse works.

Quentin releases my wrists, and I hear the zipper of his pants. He pushes my robe off my shoulders and then drags me over to the bed. The next thing I know, I'm on all fours on the mattress and he's kneeling behind me as the tip of his cock presses against my pussy.

"You're mine, even if I share you."

I moan loudly. I love this side of Quentin. He's always so controlled and gentle when we're in bed, and it's a treat for me to see this new aggressive and commanding side of him. My entire body tingles in anticipation as I wait for him to fuck me.

When he sinks his cock into me, he's slow and methodical. I moan as he stretches me with his thickness. Once he's seated deep within me, he grasps my hips firmly with both hands and slides almost completely out before slowly pressing into me again with a groan. He does it again, this time picking up the pace slightly, and I whimper in frustration. I want him to pound into me. I want him to fuck me hard.

He doesn't.

He continues to tease me with his torturous, measured strokes, making me beg for more. My voice is strained, and I know I sound desperate. "Please? Oh god, please fuck me hard?"

Quentin's hands tighten on my hips, and he pulls me backwards into his thrusts, slamming his cock deeper into my pussy but still maintaining the steady rhythm. He's in control here, and I'm not. The realization makes me feel like the ultimate fucktoy, and I love it.

My husband's tempo increases as he fucks me, and I push myself back to match his pace. My clit buzzes, and my body is wound so tightly I can hardly stand it.

Quentin groans loudly, and the sound makes me shiver in delight. I love the fact that my body belongs to him right now, and he's the one using me. He's driving me wild with desire. I want more...I need more.

He's caught up in the moment just as much as I am, and he grabs my hair with one hand and wraps it tightly around his fist before pulling my head up. The pain in my scalp sends a surge of pleasure through me as he continues to pound my pussy relentlessly.

"Oh, fuck!" I scream, "Don't stop...please."

My orgasm rips through me like a wildfire, and every nerve ending in my body comes alive at once. My pussy pulses, squeezing his cock as my muscles spasm uncontrollably.

I'm still shaking as my husband groans loudly and blows his load. I can feel his cum coating me as he shoots rope after rope inside me.

I collapse forward onto the bed with my husband draped over my back, both of us panting. Quentin's breath tickles my neck and he places a kiss there.

He murmurs, "That was so amazing, baby. Thank you."

My mind is so fucked, I can't even lift my head as I giggle. "I should be the one thanking you. I've never seen you like this before."

"Like what? Possessive?"

"Mmm, yes. I loved it."

My husband gives me a heated look. "Good, because that's what happens when you let strange men touch what's mine. That phone call was the last straw. I had to be here so I could remind you who you belonged to."

A soft thrill runs through me. "I'm all yours."

Oh, yeah. He can get possessive and fuck me like that whenever he wants. We exchange smiles and lie together as we both recover. When Quentin eventually rolls off me and sits up, his eyes have a naughty twinkle in them. "So, how about you give me a tour of the resort and we see what happens?"

I giggle. "Sounds good to me."

Quentin stands up and adjusts his pants, tucking his cock away. He holds out his hand to me, and I take it, letting him pull me to a sitting position.

I'm dressed in record time—choosing a sundress with no bra or panties, because what's the point? Sliding my feet into my sandals, I follow Quentin out the door. We hold hands as we walk toward the beach and I point things out about the resort. My pink and black wristbands keep catching my attention, and I notice Quentin glancing at them a couple of times. Neither of us says it out loud, but

I can tell we're both wondering how long it'll be before someone uses me.

We pass a few couples on the path, and they smile, but no one tries to talk to us. When we come to some rockery steps with a railing that leads down to a sandy path to the beach, we pause for a moment. Coming up the steps in our direction are two guys.

I assume they won't mess with me since Quentin and I look to be heading somewhere with purpose. We're only a few steps down when they get to us. I gasp in surprise when one of them grabs my wrist and pulls me down another step before bending me over the railing.

The guy addresses my husband. "Sorry dude, just gonna unload. I'll only be a moment."

When Quentin laughs and says, "Have fun," a naughty zing of joy heads straight to my clit.

I grasp the railing with both hands as the guy lifts me off my feet and tips me forward so he can enter me at the right angle.

I moan as his cock slides into me, and I look over my shoulder to see my handsome husband watching with rapt attention and a bulge beneath his jeans. My pussy clenches at my husband's expression, and the man fucks me slowly, as if he's got all the time in the world. Not too long ago, I didn't even know what freeuse was, and now I think I've found my favorite kink. I'm just a slut who wants a bunch of guys to fuck me whenever they want, and having my husband here watching doubles my pleasure.

I can feel the bliss building in layers, and right before I can orgasm, the guy fucking me grunts and thrusts into me hard as he comes, shooting his load deep inside me. I can feel it filling me and spilling out, running down my thighs.

The man eases me down to my feet and pulls my dress over my ass before slapping it and walking away. The other guy gives me a smile before joining his buddy as they continue past us to head toward the main building.

Quentin steps close behind me, and I can feel his hard cock against my lower back through his jeans. He wraps his hand around me, pulls my dress up with one hand, and slides the other one down my stomach and between my legs. He rubs the sticky mix of cum and my juices around, sliding his fingers inside my pussy to tease me while my mind whirls from ecstasy.

I moan as Quentin whispers huskily, "Did you like that, baby? Did you like being fucked by that complete stranger in front of me?"

My pussy throbs from the lack of orgasm, and I whimper without responding. My brain feels fuzzy, and I can't form a coherent answer. Instead, I rock against my husband's fingers, begging him to keep finger fucking me.

He laughs as he withdraws his finger from inside me and pushes me forward until I'm bending over the railing again. When he spreads my ass cheeks, I freeze as I realize what he's about to do. Ohhhh god. Right here? Right now? Quentin's slick finger rubs against my puckered asshole. He circles it, teasing me before he presses in gently.

Quentin's other hand moves to my clit, stroking lightly as I relax under his touch. "Do you trust me, baby?" he asks softly.

I nod as I let my head fall forward, giving in to whatever he wants to do to me.

Quentin continues to rub my clit and play with the rim of my ass while he talks to me in his sexy, soothing baritone. "I want you to enjoy all of this. I want you to experience every pleasure this place has to offer."

He's convinced me. I need someone in every hole. When he removes his hands, he helps me stand up, and I sway against him.

My voice trembles with desire. "We should go back to the room. I want the green wristband."

He chuckles and pulls the green band from his pocket. "No need."

He removes the pink and black bands on my wrist before sliding the green one over my hand, letting it rest on my skin.

I stare down at it. "When? How?"

Quentin pulls me close and kisses my forehead. "I had a hunch you were going to want more."

I can practically hear him smiling, and I'm not sure I've loved him more than I do in this moment. He knows I'm a slut at heart. This resort might be heaven on earth, but having my husband here makes it so much better. I'm going to enjoy every minute left of our trip.

"I love you," I whisper, looking up at him with adoration.

Quentin's eyes shine. "I love you too…now let's go see if someone is tempted to use you by the pool. We can see the ocean tomorrow."

I shiver with excitement when his hand slides down and cups my ass as he guides me down the path to the pool. My pussy buzzes with neediness, and the cum dripping between my legs is a reminder of how filthy I am…filthy in such a wonderful way.

The pool is deserted when we get there, and I'm about to ask Quentin what we should do, when he pulls my sundress over my head. I shiver as the warm breeze caresses my skin and my nipples harden.

"Hey, what do you think you're doing?" I tease him.

Quentin winks. "Getting you naked. I want to see your beautiful tits bounce when someone comes along and fucks you."

Oh, wow. I didn't expect that answer, and my body hums with excitement. I'm worked up, and since we're still alone, I decide to take a dip in the pool to cool off.

Kicking off my sandals, I slip into the refreshing water, moaning as the water laps at my skin. I duck under the surface, feeling the coolness envelop me. The water swirls around me, and I'm hypersensitive to even the brush of water against my sensitive areas. When I resurface, I hear Quentin groan. "Fuck...you're so sexy, baby."

My body responds instantly to his words, tingling with longing. I'm not sure who is going to join us next or where they will want to fuck me, but I'm ready for my husband to see all my holes filled. The thought sends a rush of arousal through my core, making me squirm with need.

If someone had mentioned a freeuse resort to me last week, I might have laughed and asked how you can really have freeuse if the person being used knows it's going to happen and welcomes it. But being here and waiting for someone to come along to use me is a delicious torture. It doesn't matter that I'm all-in and ready to go, just the fact that these are strangers who can walk up to me and just bend me over puts me in the mindset of complete submission to whoever wants me.

And knowing my husband is here and letting it happen? Yeah...this resort is magical.

Closing my eyes, I float on my back and enjoy the feeling of my husband's eyes on my body. I feel sexy and powerful in a way I never have before. Knowing Quentin wants to watch me get fucked by other men gives me a huge confidence boost. I feel like a total slut, and I'm embracing it.

"Wow...she looks delicious," someone says from the side of the pool, and I open my eyes.

The voice belongs to a man who is probably in his early forties. He's with two younger guys. All three are muscular and hot. Neediness swirls in my core as the guys remove their shoes and shirts. The older guy glances at Quentin before he unzips his pants. "Do you want to watch us fuck her?"

Quentin's lips curl up into a sexy smile. "Yes, I do."

The man laughs and walks to the edge of the pool while the two other guys stand and watch.

My heart beats rapidly when Quentin says, "Make her scream for more."

My entire body is thrumming with lust. Three men...this will be intense. How many cocks will I take today?

Once the older guy is naked, he joins me in the pool. The water moves around him, rippling outward as he approaches. He slips his hands under my arms and pulls me close. I'm aroused at the thought of having three cocks inside me while my husband watches, and my nipples brush against his chest as he pulls me to him and kisses me.

His kiss is rough and possessive, and I'm so engrossed in the way his body feels different from my husband's that I don't notice one of the other men got in the pool until he comes up behind me. The older guy stops kissing me and pushes on my shoulder, forcing me to lean back against the dude behind me while the older one hooks his arms around my thighs and pulls me up to his cock. I'm suspended between them in the water, and I gasp when he sinks his cock into me.

I can feel the other man's hard cock digging into my back as the older guy fucks me. The pleasure in my core intensifies, but I'm craving more. I want more than one hole filled.

As if they are reading my mind, the guys stop fucking me and both drag me out of the pool.

"It's time to make you scream for your husband."

The third guy approaches, naked as well, and he's got a bottle of lube in his hands. Oooh, god, I'm going to get what I want. The older guy moves me to a lounge chair. When he reclines, he pulls me on top of him so I'm facing him while I straddle him. He lines his cock up with my pussy and grips my waist, forcing me down on his cock.

Bracing my hands on the chair behind his head, he fucks me furiously. I'm in a daze as one of the others moves behind me and spreads my ass cheeks apart. Oh god...this is it. My body hungers for more as a lubed finger brushes against my ass and slowly sinks in.

I whimper, "Oh...fuck," as I press against his finger eagerly as he prepares me for his cock. As good as what he's doing feels, I'm craving something thicker. When he replaces his fingers with the head of his cock, I almost cheer.

My breathing quickens as he slowly pushes inside me, pausing every few seconds to give me time to adjust to his size. I've never had two cocks at once, and the pleasure of both of them inside me is mind blowing as fiery sparks shoot across my body.

Once he's fully seated, he thrusts into me gently as he sets a rhythm with the guy in my pussy. Each thrust from either of them makes me moan and whimper as delight swirls in my core. I close my eyes, letting the bliss course through every inch of me.

They sync up, pounding into my holes at a rapid pace. The full feeling is so intense, I can't hold in my moans of delight. I can't believe my husband wants me to do this and is watching. I'm married to the most wonderful guy ever for giving me the chance at this much pleasure.

My whole body feels like it's on fire as they continue fucking me. I'm reeling towards ecstasy, and I lose all sense of time as I transcend to a higher plane of joy. Every stroke feels like an eternity, as my body coils, ready to explode.

When the third guy stands next to us and something pushes against my cheek, I open my eyes to see a massive cock waiting for me. Turning towards him, I hum with happiness as my lips stretch around his girth.

He slides down my throat and says, "Good slut...swallow it all."

Mmm, I am a good slut. He rocks into my mouth, and for a minute I revel in the feeling of being completely stuffed. This is exactly what I was hoping would happen, and it makes me feel like I'm just a hole for them to use. The pleasure they're giving me is secondary to the illicit naughtiness of having three guys at once.

I'm almost surprised when the cock in my mouth pulses and the salty taste of his cum coats my tongue. I moan as he shoots more cum down my throat. Fuuuck, this is dirty.

I'm trying to swallow it all down when the cock in my ass suddenly slams against me harder, sending ripples of delight through me. I moan around the cock I'm trying to suck clean as I climax. The orgasm rushes through me in waves before the guy in my pussy rubs my clit, and I peak again. I scream in joy, and my body shudders violently as every muscle contracts. I'm tingling from ecstasy as the guys hammer into me again and again before finally erupting inside both holes.

The world spins, and my vision blurs as their hot cum fills me. Everyone groans as they unload, and I try to imagine what this looks like for my husband. He's got one filthy wife.

It takes a moment for my breathing to return to normal, but when I come back down from the intense high, I feel like I'm floating on a cloud of pure rapture.

"Holy fuck…" I whisper as they slide out of me, one by one.

Within seconds, Quentin pulls me off the guy and wraps me in his arms. He runs his fingers through my hair, tilting my face toward him as he says huskily, "Baby, that was so amazing to watch."

He doesn't give me time to respond before he swings me into his arms and carries me away from the pool. I hear him saying goodnight and thanking the guys as I float along in my happy place. I can tell by Quentin's determined steps he's going to fuck me as soon as we get into our room.

I'm not wrong.

Quentin shuts the door with a foot and strides across the floor straight to the bed. He lays me down gently and doesn't waste any time as he climbs onto the bed and kisses me. His lips move against mine hungrily, as if he wants to devour me, and I sigh in pleasure. When he cups my breast and pulls on the nipple gently, I almost giggle when I realize I'm still naked. I guess my sundress is still at the pool.

He continues to kiss me as he runs his hand over my body. When he slides a hand between my legs and circles my clit with his finger, I moan softly into his mouth, wishing this could go on forever. I need his gentleness after such an intense fucking.

When we break apart, my husband whispers softly, almost like a prayer, "My beautiful slutty wife...that was incredible."

I smile at him as he fumbles with his pants to get his cock out while he continues talking. "You looked so stunning filled by three cocks at once. Your expression was pure bliss."

Mmm, his praise is filthy and I love it. When he settles between my legs, I moan as he slides into me and fucks me slowly. My eyes roll back from delight, and knowing he still loves me after seeing me fucked by multiple guys is a heady feeling.

The orgasm builds inside me as he fucks me faster and harder. When he groans, "God, I love you," the bliss peaks and rushes through me, flooding me with pleasure and washing away everything but this moment with him.

When he feels me coming, it pushes him over the edge, and he cries out with his release, adding another load of cum deep inside me to mix with the other guys' seed. He hammers into me, unloading everything he's got until he shivers and slumps on top of me.

As the rapture fades, Quentin kisses me sweetly before rolling to the side and pulling me close. My head is still swirling from so many orgasms today, but I need to make sure he knows how I feel.

"I love you so much," I whisper. "Thank you for a wonderful trip."

His smile is full of love and admiration, and he kisses me again and murmurs, "You're welcome, baby."

If he ever suggests another freeuse resort trip, I'll jump at the chance but only if he wants to watch again. Life really can't get any better than this.

The End

MY HUSBAND HELPS SOMEONE USE ME

I was wrong. It could get better.

I'm not sure how long I was asleep, but the smell of something delicious wakes me up and my stomach rumbles. My husband is setting a tray of food on the table in our bungalow when I open my eyes.

Looking over at me, he smiles and says, "Hey, beautiful. You're awake."

I stretch and tease him. "Someone spoiled me with mind-blowing orgasms all day. How long did I sleep?"

Quentin laughs. "Just for a couple of hours, but with your workout earlier, you need to eat."

My stomach rumbles and I laugh. Yeah, I need food.

I climb out of bed, sore in all the right places, and wrap a robe around me while I investigate the feast he brought. Oooh...this looks so good. There's a chicken breast with a white sauce drizzled over it, roasted baby red potatoes, and a side salad.

The patio door is open, and a gentle sea breeze reminds me why I love living in Hawaii. We eat in silence, each lost in our thoughts, and a jolt of arousal surges through me as I remember all the guys I fucked earlier. Hell, I don't even know the count. This resort is amazing. My friend Mandy isn't going to believe the story I tell her when I get home.

When we're done eating, I take a quick shower, and while I'm drying my hair, I hear Quentin talking to someone in the bedroom. I assume he's on the phone with work, so I don't bother putting a robe on as I join him in the bedroom. When I spot a tall figure out of the corner of my eye, I almost trip in surprise.

The guy smiles at me, dimples flashing.

Hey, it's Dimples!

My entire body flushes as I remember what he did to me earlier. I'm about to ask him what he's doing here when he approaches me and pushes me up against the dresser. Oh, hello there. His kiss is fierce and hungry, leaving no doubt how much he wants me. He leans me backwards, grasps both wrists with one hand, and pins them to the wall above my head while his other hand goes straight to my pussy. I spread my legs and moan into his mouth as his fingers brush against my clit before he shoves two of them inside me and finger fucks me fast. It only takes a few strokes for me to feel an orgasm starting to build.

Holy fuck, what a hello. I love how these guys at the resort just take what they want without hesitation. He finger fucks me as pleasure swirls low in my stomach until Quentin calls out, "Why don't you fuck her on the bed so we can both use her at once?"

Um, what did my husband just say?

Dimples lifts his head, his eyes sparkling with lust. "Excellent idea."

When he releases my wrists, he pulls me off the dresser and hauls me over to the bed.

"On your hands and knees, slut," he demands.

He pulls his cock out of his jeans while I scramble to obey. Holy shit, this is crazy and amazing.

Once I'm in position, he grasps my hips and rubs his cock up and down my wet slit. My core floods with anticipation as he slides just the tip of his cock into me, groaning loudly. "God, you feel so good."

I wiggle my ass at him impatiently and moan, "Fuck me, please."

Quentin climbs onto the bed in front of me, completely naked. He's fully erect, and I can feel my mouth water as I picture myself sucking on him while getting fucked. Yep, this trip totally got better.

I'm distracted by Quentin and not prepared when Dimples slams his cock into me. I cry out as my pussy stretches around him, and it feels so good I push backwards until he's fully seated inside me. God, I love having an enormous cock inside me.

Quentin gets my attention when he moves his cock towards my mouth. I stick my tongue out eagerly to taste his delicious pre-cum, and my husband grins down at me as he brushes the tip of his cock across my lips before sliding between them. Oh god...I can't believe how filthy this is.

Sucking on my husband while someone else fucks me is something I never dared to imagine would happen.

Quentin groans softly as he slides down my throat while Dimples picks up speed and fucks me harder as he pants, "Jesus, your wife's pussy is a dream."

Him talking about me like I'm not even here makes me feel like a sex toy. My mind drifts into fantasy mode, where it's only about the guy's pleasure and not about me. I never knew how much I'd crave being used like this.

When Quentin tilts his head back and closes his eyes, losing himself in the moment, I focus on sucking him hard while bobbing my head. I swallow more of him as my cheeks hollow with suction. I want to make sure he gets as much pleasure as he can since he's so damn wonderful for arranging this trip. Quentin's cock glides across my tongue, and I taste more of his pre-cum as Dimples jackhammers into my pussy. Each thrust from behind shoves my husband's shaft further down my throat. I'm taking both their cocks like a champ. I feel like I was made for this.

When Dimples speeds up, I can feel the intense bliss building in my core. I suck harder on Quentin's cock, and my toes curl as delight ripples through me. An extra sharp whack against my pussy tips me over the edge, and

Quentin's cock muffles my cries of delight as an orgasm blasts through me.

As soon as the bliss fades, another orgasm takes its place. Fuck...they are peaking, one after the other, until I can't keep track. I'm completely lost to the overwhelming euphoria. Everything narrows down to this moment in time—this rapturous pleasure that pulses within every inch of me and sets me ablaze. All I am is a sex goddess made of pure sensation.

Dimples comes, and I shudder again as his cock jerks and twitches inside me while he coats my walls with his seed. He slows down and fucks his cum back into me as Quentin groans and blows his load in my throat. It's a powerful rush being used by them both at once.

The guys pull out, and I collapse onto the bed, face down. I can feel the cum leaking from my pussy as I lick my lips to clean my mouth up. Quentin sits on the bed and brushes my hair from my face, and I giggle at how fucked I am. Jesus, now I really don't think this day can get any better.

"I'm heading out," Dimples says, and I glance back at him, admiring the actual dimples in his cheeks again when he smiles.

"Thanks for stopping in," I say with another giggle. Oh yeah, I'm fucked.

My husband says, "Glad I ran into you in the dining room. This was fun."

"Yeah, thanks for inviting me," Dimples replies on his way out.

Oh shit, that's how Dimples got here. My head is foggy from satisfaction, but knowing Quentin coordinated this all makes it hotter. I get up on my hands and knees so I can kiss him sweetly. When our lips touch, warmth spreads through me and happiness fills me from head to toe.

We only kiss for a moment before he pulls me down onto the bed next to him so we can snuggle and relax. Quentin deserves an award for being such a wonderful husband.

Best. Trip. Ever.

The End

Want a free hotwife story? Join my newsletter at:
https://www.lacey-cross.net/bonusfreeusehallpass

About Lacey Cross

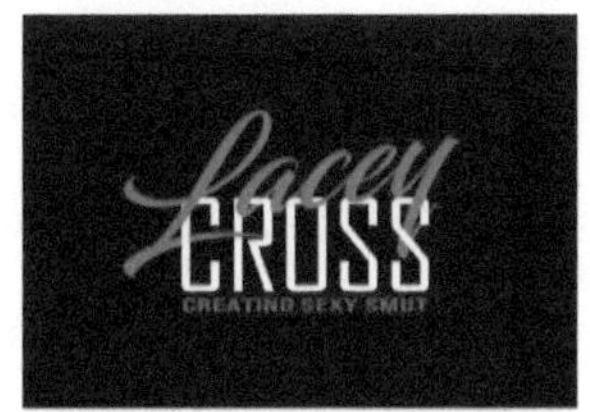

Lacey Cross is a wife sharing erotica writer with over 100 short stories published since she started in 2021. Her stories emphasize the pleasure found from the wife living her best slut life and embracing the hotwife lifestyle. She explores themes of free use, submissive wives with dominant bulls, BDSM...and oh-so-many men.